W9-BFI-053

Pigboy

Vicki Grant

Orca currents

ORCA BOOK PUBLISHERS

Library and Archives Canada Cataloguing in Publication

Grant, Vicki

Pigboy / Vicki Grant

(Orca currents)

ISBN 10: 1-55143-666-3 (bound) ISBN 10: 1-55143-643-4 (pbk.)
ISBN 13: 978-1-55143-666-1 (bound) ISBN 13: 978-1-55143-643-2 (pbk.)

I. Title. II Series.

PS8613.R367P53 2006   jC813'.6   C2006-903444-3

Summary: A school field trip to a heritage farm turns dangerous when
an escaped convict appears on the scene.

First published in the United States, 2006
Library of Congress Control Number: 2006928966

Orca Book Publishers gratefully acknowledges the support for its publishing
programs provided by the following agencies: the Government of Canada
through the Book Publishing Industry Development Program and the
Canada Council for the Arts, and the Province of British Columbia
through the BC Arts Council and the Book Publishing Tax Credit.

Cover design: Doug McCaffry
Cover photography: Getty Images

Orca Book Publishers
PO Box 5626, Station B
Victoria, BC Canada
V8R 6S4

Orca Book Publishers
PO Box 468
Custer, WA USA
98240-0468

www.orcabook.com
Printed and bound in Canada.
010 09 08 07 • 6 5 4 3

*For the wonderful Maggie deVries,
with thanks for getting me hooked
on writing books. V.G.*

chapter one

A farm.

No. It was worse than that.

A "heritage" farm.

A big, fat, stinking—and I do mean stinking—heritage farm. No running water. No electricity. No pop machine.

I couldn't believe it.

The other class went to a television studio for their field trip. They got to look through the cameras and talk to the announcers. One kid even got to read the weather forecast on the news. How cool is that?

Our class, on the other hand, was going to a stupid farm somewhere out in the sticks.

Is that fair?

I don't know why I was even surprised. What else would you expect from a guy like Mr. Benvie? There's no way he'd actually do something fun. He's a big Mr. Do-gooder. He spent his entire summer building a well in this village in Africa.

Good for him.

I mean it. I'm not just saying it.

It's really nice all those people aren't dying anymore. It's great they have water to grow their crops and feed their animals and stuff like that.

But that doesn't mean that farming is actually interesting.

That doesn't mean that anybody around here actually cares where food comes from.

That doesn't mean that any normal

teenager would actually want to waste an entire day at some stupid boring farm.

Mr. Benvie's a teacher. He spends his whole life with kids. He should have known that.

I mean, what's wrong with the guy? Clearly, any field trip involving manure is not right for a bunch of fourteen-year-olds.

But manure wasn't even the worst part of the stupid field trip.

The worst part was that the farmer grows pigs. And pigs are also called hogs. And there's this poor guy in our class called Dan Hogg who everybody hated.

I don't know why exactly. Maybe it was his hair. Or his teeth. Or his glasses. Or the fact that he answered Mr. Benvie's questions as if he might actually have a brain. Usually he just tried to sort of disappear, but it never worked. Idiots like Shane Coolen or Tyler March wouldn't take their eyes off him. They wouldn't shut up about him. They wouldn't quit laughing at him.

That's what really bugged me. Mr. Benvie saw what was going on. If he was such a good guy, why did he go and make it worse? He was all concerned about these people who live a million miles away. But he didn't seem to mind torturing some poor kid in his own class by telling everyone that we're going to see "how chickens, cows and *hogs* are traditionally raised."

That was too much for Shane. He yelled, "Visiting some of your relatives, are we, Dan? I always wanted to meet your mother."

Ha-ha-ha.

Everyone cracked up. Mr. Benvie said, "All right, that's enough," but I could tell he had trouble not laughing too.

I hated Shane Coolen.

I hated stupid field trips.

But, most of all, I hated being Dan Hogg.

chapter two

The day of the field trip, Mr. Benvie had the stomach flu. I was so happy when I found out.

I figured there was no way we'd be going to that stupid farm now. I couldn't believe my luck. I'd been up all night worrying about how I'd survive seven hours of hog jokes. I practically jumped for joy when the principal said Mr. Benvie would be out for a couple of days. Maybe, I thought, by the time he got better, he'd have come to his senses. Maybe he'd let us do something else instead. Visit the tire factory or see one of those boring history movies or go to the fire station. Anything but that stupid farm and its pigpens.

For a while, it looked like I might actually make it through the day.

Then there was a knock at the door, and the principal introduced our substitute teacher. I saw the rubber boots she was wearing. I just knew what was coming next. The principal put on this big phony smile and went, "Ms. Creaser is delighted to be able to accompany 9B on your exciting trip to historic Windmill Farm!"

He blabbed on about how the farmer had come from Holland to raise these special old-fashioned animals. Apparently it was all very fascinating—but I wasn't listening.

All I could think was, I knew it.

Why did I even hope the trip would be cancelled? Something that good would never happen to me. I'm just not a lucky person.

Whenever I'd say that to my mother she'd go, "Oh! That's nonsense! Of course you're lucky. You're young. You're healthy. You have a roof over your head and food to eat." As if that was going to make me feel better. It just made me feel pathetic.

Basically, she was saying I'm lucky because I'm not dead.

I looked around the class. Why couldn't I be lucky the way these other kids are lucky? They're young and healthy too—but they also get to be tall and good-looking and funny and rich and athletic and popular, and all the other things I have no hope of ever being.

If I ever said that to my mother, she'd just shake her head and tell me how much worse off I could be. I'm a scrawny buck toothed nerd named Hogg. "Imagine," she'd say, "how much worse it is to be an overweight Hogg like your cousin Andy. Imagine what he has to go through."

Right. I could just picture it. Next time that idiot Shane bugged me about my name I'd say, "Well, at least, I'm not a fat Hogg."

And next time he mentioned my buckteeth, I'd point out that at least I have teeth.

And if he ever brought up the fact again that I could start fires with my coke-bottle glasses, I'd explain how handy that would be if we wanted to have a wienie roast one day.

I almost laughed when I thought of that, but I could feel Shane looking at me. Only losers laugh to themselves.

The principal was still yakking away about traditional hog farming. Shane was still whispering stupid jokes to his friends and cracking up. How could my mother think I was lucky?

I wasn't even lucky enough to get the flu when I needed it.

chapter three

People were pushing and shoving for a good spot, but I managed to get a seat by myself in the back of the bus.

Big surprise.

I always got a seat by myself. The boys thought I was weird. The girls didn't think about me at all. No one ever wanted to sit with me. I didn't care. I was used to it.

The bus driver said it would take about an hour to get to the farm. That was okay.

I could sleep. I was tired after being up the night before. I was going to need all my strength to make it through the rest of the day. It takes a lot of energy to act like those idiots don't bother me.

Ms. Creaser was talking to some girls up front. They were having quite a little conversation. Something about her jacket. I guess they liked it, the way they were squealing about it. Ms. Creaser was pretty young and dressed like a VJ—other than the rubber boots, that is. She reminded me of my half sister and her college friends. You know, the clothes, the earrings, the big laugh.

I didn't want to act like a weirdo, so I stopped watching them and just looked out the window. There wasn't much else to do.

Boring.

For a while there were houses and, every so often, someone out walking a dog. Once we got on the highway, though, there were just 18-wheelers and gas stations. It was even worse after we turned on to a country road. We passed this dead little village, a couple of farms—and then there was nothing.

No houses. No fields. Not even any signs. Just miles and miles of the worst dirt road you ever saw.

Every time we went over a bump I thought, I'm going to be sick. That was all I needed. If I threw up on the bus, my life would be worthless. They'd never let me forget it. Seriously. Never.

My mother told me to take a carsickness pill before I left. She kept saying I'd be sorry. I hate it when she treats me like a kid. I didn't take one. I hoped it wasn't too late to take one now.

I rooted around in my backpack. I found allergy pills, Kleenex, duct tape—all the stuff you'd expect a nerd like me to have—but nothing for carsickness.

We went over another bump, and it was all I could do not to heave. I closed my eyes and told myself not to think about it.

That was a lot easier than I thought it was going to be.

A second later, my face was smashed up against the bus window. I heard the arm to my glasses snap off and that stupid laugh of his. On the plus side, I completely forgot about throwing up.

Shane Coolen gave me a big yellow smile and said, "Mind if I join you, Pigboy?"

chapter four

Mr. Benvie bugged me, but I had to say this for him: Whenever we went on a field trip, he always sat at the back of the bus. There was no way he'd ever let Shane and Tyler out of his sight.

I should have thought about that before I chose my seat. I should have found a place up front near Ms. Creaser. I would have looked like a chicken, but at least I wouldn't have had two hundred pounds of Shane Coolen slamming me into the side of the bus.

"Scooch over!" he said in this fake girly voice. "A little more...A little more... Attaboy. I'm not squishing you now, am I?"

What was I supposed to say?

If I said yes, he'd pound me for being a wuss. If I said no, he'd crush me until I said yes—then he'd pound me.

I couldn't win. I just kept my mouth shut and hoped that the lenses of my glasses wouldn't break. I'd be blind without them. I could probably have lived with that—but what would I tell my mother? I didn't need her finding out about this. If Shane thought I was running home to my mama like some little wimp, he'd really torture me.

Shane had his feet pushed up against the arm of the seat and was leaning against my back like I was a beanbag chair. Every time he moved, that little metal rim around the window dug deeper into my face. I could taste the blood from my nose dripping into my mouth. I wondered how much longer my teeth would last.

Shane took my arm and bent it back at the elbow. He started going, "This little piggy went to market. This little piggy went home..." Tyler and his buddies were cracking up. I could hear them snorting.

I was worried about what Shane had in store for the last little piggy—when everyone suddenly stopped laughing. Shane hopped up and moved over to his side of the seat.

Ms. Creaser was heading to the back of the bus.

Shane, like, hissed at me, "Keep your face down!" Then he started whistling. What an idiot. If Ms. Creaser didn't think he was guilty before, she sure did when he started doing that zippity-do-dah stuff. He was trying way too hard to look innocent.

"What happened here?" she said.

Shane shrugged and went, "Huh? What do you mean? I've just been enjoying the scenery. Nothing happened that I know of."

"Nothing?" she said. "Then why's your friend here bleeding?"

Shane went, "Oh, right! Sorry, I forgot about that." He patted me on the back. "Daniel has a nosebleed. He gets them all the time, poor guy." Another one of those big yellow smiles.

Ms. Creaser leaned over and lifted my chin. She looked at me and my bloody face and my broken glasses, then she looked at Shane. She looked at Shane for a long, long time. After a while, he stopped smiling. You could tell she thought he was an idiot.

She said, "I don't suppose you're the famous Mr. Coolen now, are you?"

He clicked his tongue and winked at her. Who did he think he was? Brad Pitt?

"Yup," he said. "That's me. The famous Mr. Coolen!"

"It's nothing to be proud of," she said. "You and I and the principal are going to have a little talk later."

"I'm looking forward to it," he said. "Not as much as I am," she said. Then she waved for me to come with her.

She smiled at me and went, "And you are Mr....?"

That was just too good to be true.

"Why, that's Mr. Hawgg!" Shane screamed out in this dumb goofball accent.

Everyone cracked up. Ms. Creaser sighed and shook her head. It was nice she was so disgusted, but it didn't help much. Even from the front of the bus I could hear Shane going, "Sooey! Sooey!"

It was going to be a long, long day.

chapter five

Ms. Creaser did her best to help. She told me about a friend of hers whose last name was Outhouse and another guy whose real name was Donald Duck. She swore it was true. I think she was just trying to be nice. She made me squeeze my nostrils together to stop the bleeding and got out the first-aid kit.

I guess most of the kids who go on

field trips are little, because the bus driver only had Cookie Monster Band-Aids. Ms. Creaser used one to put my glasses back together. I was too embarrassed to tell her I had duct tape in my backpack. Only a jerk would carry duct tape around with him.

The bleeding wouldn't stop, so she got me to stuff some Kleenex up my nostrils.

Could my life get any worse?

Coke bottle glasses held together by a Cookie Monster Band-Aid. Kleenex stuffed up a bloody nose. Swollen lips over buckteeth. At least I didn't smell bad. I knew it was going to be a stressful day. I really piled on the deodorant.

Ms. Creaser asked me about my hobbies and my friends. I made some stuff up so she wouldn't feel any worse for me than she already did. I didn't mind talking to her. She was pretty nice. We were at the farm before I knew it.

The bus pulled into the yard. A bunch of geese flew off in a panic. Some goats turned around and looked at us. Clearly, an actual motor vehicle was a big deal around here.

The farm sure didn't look like much. The house was okay, I guess. It looked like the kind of house you'd see in a picture book. It was white with a black roof and had windows with those little crosses in them. There was a green door right in the middle, a few flowers in the front. It was nothing special.

Everything else was pretty ratty. The fences were made of old logs leaning on top of each other. The barn was unpainted and missing a bunch of boards up top. Other than that, there were just some animals in pens, a skuzzy pond and an old log building out past the barn. I figured it was going to be pretty hard to find something to do around here for the next four hours. I hated the thought of Shane having time on his hands.

Ms. Creaser stood at the front of the bus and gave everyone their orders. She made that usual teacher's speech about how we're ambassadors for the school. "I expect you all to be on your best behavior." She looked right at Shane when she said that.

"Oh, you can count on me, Ms. Creaser!" he said.

"Yup," she said. "I know that. And that's why you can count on me watching you." Then she reminded us to leave our backpacks on the bus and told us to file out.

I should have grabbed my allergy pills and my Kleenex, but I was too embarrassed. I was right at the front, and everyone was piled up behind me waiting to get out. I covered my face with my hand and turned my head like I was going to sneeze. I didn't want anyone to see. I shoved the Kleenex up my nose so it wouldn't show and got out of the bus.

Ms. Creaser knocked on the farmhouse door. I tried to stay as close to her as I could without looking like I was trying to stay close to her. I'd rather get pounded for being myself than get pounded for being a teacher's pet.

She knocked again. No answer. She looked in the little windows that ran down the side of the door and shrugged.

"He must be in the barn," she said. The kids were all using this little setback as a chance to goof around, but she wasn't going for it. She just stared at them and they all stopped.

"Okay," she said. "C'mon, you guys. Keep up."

Everyone did what they were told. That was pretty strange. Ms. Creaser was just a substitute teacher. Usually, the class went crazy when we had substitutes—but everyone listened to her. I don't know why. She wasn't big and mean and possibly insane like that Mr. Laffoley we had once. He managed to keep everyone under control but only because we were terrified. Even Shane shut up.

Ms. Creaser was actually kind of little. Not short really—but thin. Half the class was bigger than her. She sure couldn't force anyone into doing what she said. She didn't need to. There was just something about the way she said stuff. People listened.

We followed her to the barn.

Other than the cows, it was deserted too. It was dark inside except for this stream of sunlight that came in through the grubby windows. You could see those little dust things dancing around in the light. Just looking at them made my nose itch. I hoped those wads of Kleenex would stop the sneezing or I was in big trouble.

Ms. Creaser stepped into the barn like it was haunted or something.

She called out, "Mr. van Wart?... Hello?...Mr. van Wart?"

Nothing.

Nothing except, of course, for Shane laughing.

Ms. Creaser came storming out of the barn.

"What's so funny?" she said.

"Funny?" he went. "I'm not laughing. I'm *concerned*. I'm just worried about Mr. van...*WART*." He screwed up his face and said "Wart" like he was going to throw

23

up—then he started to laugh again. People snickered, but nobody came right out and laughed with him.

You should have seen the look on Ms. Creaser's face. She went right up to him. She didn't care that he was about a foot taller and a hundred pounds bigger than she was.

"You listen to me," she said. "You might be too immature to understand this, but I'm telling you anyway. Mr. van Wart is Dutch. His name is Dutch. It doesn't mean the same thing in English as it does in Dutch. He is also our host. If you make one more of your silly jokes or so much as crack a smile when I introduce him, you will be very, very sorry. Have I made myself clear?"

Shane had a smirk on his face, but he didn't say anything. He just nodded.

Ms. Creaser turned to the rest of us. "Mr. van Wart might have a thick accent. If you have trouble understanding him, I'll try and step in. Got it? Okay—now, best behavior," she said.

She went around behind the barn.

She was going, "Mr. van Wart! Mr. van Wart!"

These big, fat, spotted pigs all started grunting and snorting like they were answering her. Shane knew better than to come right out and laugh, but I knew he loved it. I knew he loved the idea of hogs making gross noises and rolling around in their own manure. I'd hear all about it the next day for sure. There was no way he was going to let me forget it.

"He's not here," Ms. Creaser said and led everyone away from the pigs. She gave me this lame smile. I think she was kind of embarrassed for me. You know, that whole hog thing.

She looked around. "I don't see him in the field either," she said. "If he's not in that log building over there, we may have to find something else to do today..."

There was a big whoop of excitement over that. She waved everyone quiet and started calling for Mr. van Wart again. A couple of seconds later, the door to the log house opened. Everyone groaned. It wasn't just me. Ms. Creaser swung around, ready to clobber us. We shut up. She turned back.

"Mr. van Wart?" she said.

He locked the door behind him, then he said, "Who are you?"

He looked kind of mad—and he didn't look much like a farmer either. I expected some old guy in a straw hat and overalls. He had the overalls, but he wasn't old. He looked like he was in his thirties. His head was shaved. He had tattoos on his knuckles. I don't know why I was surprised—I mean, who says farmers can't have tattoos?—but I was.

"I'm Ms. Creaser. I'm sorry. You must have been expecting Mr. Benvie," she said. "He would have loved to come, but he's got the flu."

The guy didn't say anything. No "that's too bad" or "give him my best" or anything like that. Mr. Benvie said they were friends, but the guy looked like he couldn't care less. After a while, Ms.

Creaser just started talking again.

"The class has been learning about traditional agriculture, and we're all thrilled that you invited us to tour your farm." That was stretching it a bit. I mean, I for one was not thrilled to be there. She smiled at him again. He just nodded.

"How did you get here?" he said.

"By bus," Ms. Creaser said. You could tell she was wondering what she'd got herself into.

"How long are you staying?" he said.

"Well, we have to be back at the school by 3:15 so we'll leave about 2:00."

The guy nodded again. He looked at us. He looked at the bus. He chewed on a wad of something. He didn't say anything for a long time. It was like he was figuring out what to do with us.

He spat.

"Okay," he said after a while. "Let's go." He finally smiled. At least he was trying.

His tour really sucked. I thought at first that it was a language thing, but after a while I realized that wasn't the problem.

He didn't have an accent. He spoke English as well as we did.

We walked through the barn. He was going, "That's a shovel. That's a pitchfork. That's a cat..."

Seriously. That's what he was doing. I mean, how stupid did he think us city kids were? Like we wouldn't know what a cat was? Everyone was rolling their eyes and sighing. Ms. Creaser glared at us.

She tried to make the tour more interesting. We walked by these cows, and she asked how old they are when they start producing milk.

The guy went, "Eighteen."

Ms. Creaser said, "Really? Eighteen years old? I didn't think cows lived that long."

She was just surprised. She didn't say he was lying or anything—but he swung around with this look on his face like he wanted to kill her.

"What?" he went. "You think I don't know what I'm talking about? That what you're saying? Huh?" He swore under his breath. We all heard him. We were totally shocked.

You don't talk to Ms. Creaser like that.

Everyone went quiet and just stared at the guy. Ms. Creaser was all red in the face. She was smiling, but it wasn't a nice smile.

She said, "Excuse me, Mr. van Wart, do you mind if we talk outside for a moment?"

I wouldn't have wanted to go outside with that guy, but Ms. Creaser held the door open like he was a kid in trouble. They both left. She closed the door behind her.

All I could think about was getting stuck here in the dark with Shane and that pitchfork. Everyone was buzzing about how Ms. Creaser was really going to give it to van Wart. I hoped that would keep Shane occupied until she got back. I edged closer to Anna McCrae, just in case. She's the nicest girl in class and pretty too. Shane usually tried to act halfway human around her.

They were gone a long time. Shane had just made his first hog joke—"Anyone feel like a pig roast?"—when the door opened.

The guy walked in. He was all red in the face. I figured he was embarrassed about being such a jerk.

"Your teacher isn't feeling well," he said. "I'm in charge now."

He smiled.

"Now we can have some real fun," he said.

chapter six

At first people were kind of nervous. Everyone was asking what was wrong with Ms. Creaser and saying maybe we should just go home and can we see her and stuff like that.

I was afraid the guy was going to blow up again. He looked kind of irritated. But he just rubbed his head with his hands a few times and asked everyone to quiet down.

His face changed. He sounded almost nice.

He said, "Look...Ah...I owe you an apology. See, I wasn't really expecting you guys. I got a lot of stuff to do today. I got a little stressed out when you showed up." He gave this weird shrug. I almost felt sorry for him. You could tell it was hard for him to say this stuff.

He looked at the ground and just sort of blurted the rest out. "I apologized to your teacher and promised to manage my anger better. She thanked me and everything was going good, but then she didn't feel so hot anymore. I told her— don't worry; I'll look after you guys. She thought that was real nice."

He looked up and smiled. He had a gold tooth.

"We'll let her lie down for a while," he said, "and then why don't we..."

I never found out what he planned to do with us. Before the guy could say another word, my allergies kicked in. Kicked in big-time.

I'd been trying my best not to sneeze, but there was so much hay and dust and grossness in that barn that I knew it was going to happen sooner or later. I tensed my whole body. I squeezed my nostrils together. I held my breath and scrunched up my face.

It didn't do any good.

The sneeze was like a rocket. It started in my gut and worked its way up my back and into my eyes and nose. I couldn't hold it anymore. It exploded out my face.

It was so loud these girls screamed as if they were being attacked by a pit bull. The worst thing was those wads of Kleenex shot right across the barn like two bloody little bullets.

For a second, nobody could figure out what had happened. There was complete silence, then somebody took a closer look at the Kleenex and realized what it was. People groaned and pointed and shrieked. Everyone turned around and stared at me with this "Ewww" look on their faces.

I said, "Excuse me," which was

apparently hilarious. What else was I supposed to say?

I just stood there feeling gross and stupid until the guy screamed, "*SHUT UP!*"

Somebody in the back was trying not to laugh, but everybody else shut up pretty fast. I felt another sneeze starting. This one was going to be even worse than the last one. It was going to be messy. I could just tell. I raised my hand.

"What do you want?" he said. He said it like he'd just about had enough of me.

I squeaked out, "Is there a washroom I could use?"

"I dunno," he said.

The principal said Mr. van Wart had only been in the country a few years. Still, you'd think that was plenty of time for him to figure out if there was a washroom on his property.

I probably should have realized something was up then, but my mind was totally out-of-order. The new sneeze had taken over my body. It yanked my belly out and threw my head back and expelled two giant jellyfish out my nose. Then the blood started again.

Everybody screamed. People stepped back into fresh piles of manure—on purpose!—to get away from me. I just stood in the middle of this big empty circle with my head down and my arms out and all this slime gushing out my nostrils.

Even the guy was grossed out. He was having trouble managing his anger again.

"You got a problem?" he said.

"I need to get my allergy pills," I said.

"Where are they?" he said.

"In the bus," I said, trying to keep those jellyfish away from my mouth.

He went, "I told you! The bus is off limits. Your teacher's sick. We don't want to disturb her."

"I really need a Kleenex," I said. He wasn't happy.

"Who's got a Kleenex?" he said.

Nobody.

Nobody had a Kleenex. I was the only person in the whole class who ever needed to blow my nose. Figures. Shane would remind me of that little fact later.

The guy shrugged. He said, "You're gonna have to just use your sleeve."

Everyone screamed and gagged at that one.

"Okay, OKAY, *OKAY*!" he said. "Get a Kleenex in the house. You got one minute. Take any longer and I'm coming after you."

It sounded like a threat. People started to mumble.

The guy smiled. "I mean, you don't want to keep everyone waiting, do you?" he said.

He opened the door. I ran out with my head down. It was so humiliating. I would have loved to have kept running and running and to never see any of them again, but where would I go? This farm wasn't even in the sticks. It was a hundred miles past the sticks. People here went to the sticks when they were looking for excitement.

I sneezed again and my neck snapped. What good would a couple of Kleenexes do? I'd go through those in about three seconds. I'd be sneezing like this until I got home if I didn't get my allergy pills. I'd be lucky if I didn't break out in hives.

I looked back at the barn. The guy couldn't see the bus door from where he was. My backpack was right at the front. It would only take me a second to nip in and get my pills. Ms. Creaser wouldn't mind. Maybe I could even ask her if she needed anything.

I slipped around to the front of the bus. The bus driver was lying down with his head on the steering wheel.

I figured he was taking a nap—until I opened the door and saw Ms. Creaser lying face down in a pool of blood.

chapter seven

The bus driver was out cold. His arms were tied behind his back. There was a T-shirt stuffed in his mouth. It was so rude. Something you'd do to an animal. I took it out so he could breathe.

Ms. Creaser's hands were tied with the blue scarf she'd been wearing. He'd obviously hit her on the head too, but somehow it was the scarf that really scared me. It seemed particularly cruel to tie someone up with their own scarf. I don't know why I thought that, but I did. I guess I wasn't thinking straight. Everything was so weird. My body was moving all fast and jerky, but my brain was like Jello.

I pushed the hair away from Ms. Creaser's face. She had a big gash on her forehead, but she was alive. She opened her eyes a bit and groaned. I didn't know what to do. I realize now I probably should have tried to use the bus driver's radio or even run for help, but I didn't. I just sort of shook for a while and wondered what the guy was going to do when he caught me.

I needed Ms. Creaser's help.

"Are you all right?" I asked, which was kind of stupid. She was lying in a pool of blood. Clearly, she wasn't all right.

I was just about to untie her hands when I heard the guy go, "...and nobody move! I mean it! I'll be back in a second to, uh, finish our tour."

I looked out the window. He was coming after me. I tried to untie the scarf, but I couldn't get my fingers to work. I was shaking too much.

"I'll be back!" I said, though I really wasn't sure that I would be. Ms. Creaser was nice. I didn't want to leave her without any hope. I was just about out the door when I remembered the Kleenex. I grabbed some from the first-aid kit and slipped out.

I don't know how the guy missed me, but he did. I managed to run around the back end of the bus and make it look as if I was just coming from the house. I tried to sort of stroll out. You know, act casual. I don't think I looked very convincing. My legs were like gummy worms.

"I found some," I said. I waved the Kleenex in the air, but I couldn't look at him. I was so freaked out I would have given myself away. I wiped my nose.

"Took you long enough," he said. "I was starting to get worried." Then he grabbed my arm and half-pushed, half-carried me back to the barn.

"I wouldn't want you to miss the rest of the tour. We're getting to the good part," he said.

"The slaughterhouse is next."

chapter eight

The guy was still smiling when we got back to the barn. It was like he'd loosened up and was starting to enjoy himself. I knew that couldn't be good.

All I could think was, Why did Mr. Benvie decide to take us here? He knew Mr. van Wart. He told us that. He told us they got together all the time to talk about farming. Mr. Benvie must have suspected there was something wrong with him. I mean, all you had to do was look at the guy.

I'm not talking about the tattoo or the gold tooth or the shaved head. My half-sister's boyfriend has all those things and a lip ring too. He's okay. Even my grandmother likes him.

But this guy? It didn't matter how much he smiled. His eyes still gave me the creeps. I couldn't figure out how Mr. Benvie would have missed that. Had the guy been hiding it before? Had he put on a good face for Mr. Benvie just so he could lure us here and...

And what?

What was he going to do to us?

Why would he even want to do anything to a bunch of kids?

It made no sense.

The guy had the pitchfork in his hand and was smiling away like a camp counselor. He said, "All right, c'mon, everyone. Get going. Nothing much happens in the barn—but I think you're really going to find this next building interesting."

If he hadn't called one of the girls "Babydoll," he would have sounded like a regular teacher.

I was terrified. I wanted to tell someone what I saw—but who? Who could I tell? It's not like I had any friends in class. If I walked up to someone and started talking, they'd probably scream and run away. No one wanted to get near Pigboy, especially after that sneeze.

And even if someone did let me near them, I wouldn't have a chance to say anything. The guy was watching every move I made. He had a pitchfork. I didn't think he was the kind of teacher who'd let you get away with "whispering in class."

The building was just a log cabin with boarded-up windows and a wooden door. The guy unlocked it and smiled at Anna McCrae.

"After you," he said and winked.

You could feel the cold and dark pouring out the door. People kind of hesitated to go in, but he nudged them along.

"C'mon! Hurry! That's it," he said. "There's something inside I want to show you."

Everyone was almost in when Anna screamed.

"There's a man here! He's bleeding!"

Things happened really fast after that. Some kids rushed in to take a look. Others tried to get out. The guy started pushing people in with the pitchfork. Everyone was screaming and crying and scratching and panicking.

Somehow he didn't notice when I ducked down and scrambled away on my hands and knees. I ran around the side of the building. I was just waiting for him to come after me.

The guy slammed the door and pulled down the latch. He locked it with a key. Then he walked away. The screaming didn't seem to bother him at all.

It was the first time in my life I'd ever been glad I was so skinny. There was a little bush in front of me. I pushed myself flat against the side of the log building and prayed the guy couldn't see past it.

He only looked back once. There was this loud noise. I guess someone inside was trying to ram the door open. There was no way they were going to get through. The guy just laughed and kept walking.

I wanted him to keep walking. And walking. And walking.

If he left for a while, maybe I'd be able to get the door unlocked. I thought if we all stuck together, maybe we could overpower him. Who knows? Maybe Shane's mean streak would finally come in handy.

More likely, Shane would be so delighted to meet someone who *shared his interests* that he and his new little friend would overpower *us*.

The guy didn't keep walking. He leaned against the fence and pulled out a cigarette. It took him about fifteen matches to get it lit. By that time, he really needed a smoke.

He was still hauling away on the cigarette when a phone rang. I jumped—but it didn't surprise him at all. He didn't even look around for it. He pulled a barrel up beside the barn and climbed on top of it. He felt around in the gutter. He pulled out a cell phone.

"Yeah," he said. He listened for a while. I couldn't hear what the other person was saying, but I could see it was making him mad.

I'll leave the swearing out.

His face was practically purple. He said, "Don't give me a hard time! Ain't my fault. How was I supposed to call you? You were the one who said only one guy would be here!"

He listened some more.

"Well, you were wrong, weren't you?...A bunch of kids, that's who...No. Not two or three! Twenty or thirty—and a teacher and a bus driver too." He laughed. "But I took care of them. No thanks to you!"

The person on the other end of the phone said something. The guy went wild. He said,

"Don't tell me to calm down! *You* calm down! I got to get out of here fast or I'm dead. The cops are going to figure out what's up." He butted his cigarette out with his foot. "So what am I gonna do now, Genius?"

The guy was pacing around the barnyard like he was a bull about to charge. He had this weird thing happening with his neck. It was creepy. He was twitching the way people in horror movies twitch just before they morph into bloodthirsty killing freaks.

He was going, "Of course they've seen my face! How was I supposed to hide my face from thirty kids? They think I'm van Wart—or at least they did till I locked them up with him..."

I know it sounds stupid—but right until that moment I did think he was van Wart. I just figured living way out here by himself with no junk food or TV must have made him nuts. I know it would have put me over the edge.

Watching him now from my hiding place, I realized the guy didn't just have a bad day and "lose it." It must have taken him years of practice to get that crazy. Next to him, Shane looked like a Sunday-school teacher. A real amateur.

"I told ya! I can't have no witnesses," the guy was saying. "I ain't going back there."

He listened for a while and then did that weird twitchy thing again. He laughed.

"Yeah," he said. "I guess I could do that. I'm pretty good at arranging tragic accidents..."

chapter nine

I didn't like the sound of that. I didn't like the sound of that *at all*. People get hurt in accidents. People get *killed* in tragic accidents. I hated to think what the guy had planned for us.

He listened for a while more, then snapped the cell phone shut. He twitched again and disappeared down the side of the barn. I had to make a run for it. I didn't know when he'd be back—or what he'd have with him. A knife? A gun? A bomb? My imagination was going crazy.

I darted across the barnyard. My feet barely touched the ground. I crouched behind an old green wagon and caught my breath.

I couldn't see the guy, but I knew he was still behind the barn. I could hear the pigs snorting away at him. Those poor animals were sure starved for company. They went nuts when anyone came near.

The bus was closer than the house, but I was too scared to go inside it. If the guy came back around the corner, he'd see me. If he came into the bus after me, I'd have nowhere to run. I'd be dead meat.

I had to get into the house instead. Maybe there'd be a phone there. I didn't even try to hide. I just went for it. I ran as fast as I could from the back of the cart to the front of the house. Then I stopped. I stood still. I listened to hear if he'd seen me. No footsteps. Nothing. I finally took another breath. I was okay. I'd made it this far.

I opened the door. It was unlocked. I snuck into the house. It was really peaceful inside. Not just quiet—but peaceful. You knew that the person who lived here never left his clothes on the floor or played air guitar when he thought no one was looking. The place felt like an old lady's house.

I tiptoed into the living room, and I got this weird feeling. It was like I'd been there before. I knew I couldn't have been—but why did everything seem so familiar? I looked around. Wooden floor. Wooden chairs. Wooden table. One of those little rugs people make out of rags. A couple of old kerosene lamps. A fireplace.

It hit me. I knew where I'd seen this place before. In the museum. This was exactly like the "Early Colonial" room they have in the "Historic Homes" section. We get dragged there every year. All this place needed was a rope across the door and a tour guide in a long dress and an old-fashioned hat.

I knew there would be no phone in a

place like this, but that didn't stop me from looking. I guess I just couldn't give up my only hope. It was like I had two different brains, each telling me what to do. One was saying, Must find phone! Call for help! The other was going, Don't even bother! The guy lives like it's still 1895. There's no phone here! There's no Kleenex here either. Get out! Run for it!

I just sort of ran around in circles like an idiot. I didn't know who to listen to.

I probably would have run around in circles all afternoon—if I hadn't heard the back door open.

chapter ten

I looked around the living room. There was no place to hide. No big couch. No big curtains. No closet. I didn't know what to do.

Or at least my brain didn't. It was in a complete panic.

My body, though, figured things out pretty fast. It saw the fireplace. Before I knew it, I'd ducked down and squeezed myself in. I had to curl up like a cinnamon roll to fit.

I just got my left foot tucked in when the guy came barreling into the room. He was wild—cursing and sputtering. He was headed right for the fireplace. The only thing blocking his view was a little wooden table. If he looked down, I was toast.

I scrunched my eyes closed. If I was going to die, I didn't want his ugly face to be the last thing I saw. I braced myself.

Nothing happened. Or at least, nothing happened to *me*.

The guy kept cursing. He knocked everything off the mantelpiece. He kicked the little wooden table. I opened my eyes a crack. His knee couldn't have been more than six inches from my face. The guy obviously didn't know I was there.

Black, sooty dust was falling all over me. In my eyes. Up my nose. Down my shirt. Normally I'd be sneezing my face off. It dawned on me that I could start sneezing at any moment.

But I didn't sneeze. My nose didn't even twitch. I guess terror works even better than pills for stopping allergies. Frankly I'd rather take the pills any day.

I watched those big boots of his tromp around the room. He was looking for something—but not very well. You could tell he was not a patient guy. He gave up pretty quick.

"They ain't here!" he said. I realized he wasn't just swearing for the fun of it. He was talking to someone on his cell phone.

"Yeah, I told ya!" he was saying. "I found the kerosene...Yeah, and I found that too. That's not the problem! The problem is I don't have no more matches... Quit giving me a hard time! I needed a smoke, okay? Just tell me where the matches are!"

There was a pause. Then the guy slammed something against the wall. The whole house shook—me included. He banged back into the kitchen.

"WHY DIDN'T YOU TELL ME THAT BEFORE?!?"

Even over the pounding of my heart, I could hear every word he said.

"Yes, I'm in the kitchen now!...Whaddya mean 'the pantry'? How am I supposed to know what a pantry is!...Just tell me where they are! Look, you worked here. Not me. I don't know where he keeps his matches! You want me to burn the place down, I need the matches!..."

Burn the place down.

I heard the words. I understood the words. But it took a few really, really long seconds before I knew what they meant. He was going to light the log house—and everyone in it—on fire. That's why he needed the matches. That's why he was talking about kerosene. That was the tragic accident he was planning.

I could hear a chair scraping across the floor and then the guy scrambling around in the kitchen. A couple of dishes broke. You could hear him throwing stuff around. He clearly didn't care what kind of mess he left behind. After a while the noise stopped. He went, "Yeah, okay, I got 'em."

The door slammed, and then everything was quiet. He'd gone outside. I could breathe.

I wanted to find a place to hide—a REAL place to hide—and stay there until the guy was gone for good. He wouldn't miss one more kid. He wouldn't even know I was gone. He'd just burn the place down, and then he'd leave. Sooner or later the police would show up. I'd explain everything then. They'd understand.

Yeah.

They'd understand that I was a chicken. That I let my whole class die. That when I had a chance to save them, I saved myself instead.

That would suck.

I thought my life was bad before. Imagine what it would be like if I let Shane die. He'd end up the big hero. Kids who die are always heroes. No one would remember what a jerk he was, how many people he tortured, how he tortured me every day of my life. They'd forget that. I'd be the live chicken, and Shane would be the dead hero—forever and ever. I'd never live it down.

I had to at least try to do something. No one would blame me if I at least tried.

I got out of the fireplace. I snuck over to the window. I hoped the guy wouldn't be able to see me through the lace curtains.

I kept losing sight of him. The bus was in the way. But I saw a can of something over by the log house. I figured it was the kerosene. My grandmother has some at the cottage in case the power goes out. That stuff's like lighter fluid. If he sprinkled it around, the house would go up in flames like a paper bag. No one inside would have a chance. I started shaking again.

I saw the guy dragging the bus driver toward the log house. A minute later, he was back, carrying Ms. Creaser. She was struggling. He didn't seem to care.

I had to do something. I ran into the kitchen. I needed a weapon. A hammer. A frying pan. Something. I know it sounds dumb, but I had this idea that I could just sneak up behind him and hit him. I actually thought I'd be strong enough to stop him somehow.

I got into the kitchen and I saw something even better than a weapon.

The guy's cell phone.

chapter eleven

It was lying on the table beside his cigarettes. I wiped the soot off my hands and dialed. I couldn't believe it. Someone answered.

This lady's voice said, "9-1-1. What is your emergency?" It was just like on TV.

I told her—or at least I tried. I must have sounded nuts. I was terrified the guy was going to come back and murder me. Under the circumstances, it was kind of hard to think straight. I just blurted out whatever came into my head. I was sure she was going to hang up on me. The story was so crazy. It sounded like some stupid joke—even to me. Some guy kidnapped my entire class and was going to light us all on fire? Who'd believe that?

The operator did. Or at least she seemed to. She didn't say, "Yeah, right..." or tell me to quit kidding around. She just kept asking me questions.

"Try to stay calm," she said. "What is your cell phone number?"

"I don't know," I said. "It's not mine."

"That's okay," she said. "Just tell me your address then."

"You mean, my home? Where I live?" I said. What was I thinking? What an idiot. Why would she care where I lived?

"No, son," she said. She didn't laugh or make it sound like I was a moron. "Your address now. Where are you now?"

That was even worse. I had no idea where this stupid farm was. I'd paid absolutely no attention to where we were going that day. I had other things on my mind. I'd been more concerned about what Shane was going to do to me when we got there.

I tried my best to remember. I tried to remember where the principal said we were going. I'd been so mad he hadn't cancelled the trip that I'd just blanked him out. I tried to picture the permission slip we had to get our parents to sign. Who reads those things? I didn't. I tried to remember what Mr. Benvie called the stupid place.

All I could think of was that guy coming back to terminate me.

"Are you still there?" the operator said.

"Yeah," I said. "I'm here."

Where was "here"? Tell her something.

"We're at the end of a dirt road," I said. "It's off the highway."

"Which highway, son?" she said.

I didn't know. There's more than one highway?

"Try to think of something you saw along the way," she said.

Shane's yellow teeth? The metal rim around the bus window? Everyone laughing? That wouldn't help. Before that—what did I see?

"Ah...Ah...Gas stations!..." I said. "Donut shops!...Houses!...Dogs...Trees..." I was desperate. I knew exactly how stupid I sounded.

Then I had a brain wave.

"We're at a farm!" I said. "Pigs...cows, you know. No electricity. No water... Um...um..." I was just throwing stuff out, talking as fast as I could. It was like I was on a game show and the timer was ticking. What else could I tell her about this place?

How could I be so dumb? Of course. "Van Wart!" I said. "Van Wart!"

I caught a glimpse of something moving in the barnyard. The guy was coming back.

"What do you mean, son?" the operator said.

I zipped back into the living room.

"He owns it!" I said.

I could hear the back steps creak.

"What's his first name?" she said.

"I don't know!" I whispered. "Call the school. Call..."

I could have killed myself. I should have thought of that earlier. I should have just told her Gorsebrook Junior High! She could have called. The principal knew where we were. It was too late now. I didn't have time to say anything. The back door had opened.

I closed the cell phone. Hanging up was cutting her off. Who knew if I'd have a chance to call again—but I couldn't let the guy hear anything.

He was cursing again. "Where did I leave my smokes?" He knocked some stuff around in the kitchen. He gave this satisfied sigh and said, "Ah, there they are." Then he paused. Something was wrong. I could just tell. It was like the air froze.

"What the...?" he said.

He started walking toward the living room. I looked down and I knew why he was coming. He was following my footprints.

My sooty footprints.

chapter twelve

It happened so fast I didn't have time to think. I just grabbed the first thing I could find and swung. I aimed for the guy's head, but I missed. I hit him in the chest with one of those kerosene lamps.

It was almost as good. It didn't knock him out—but he went down. For a while, he even stayed down. He was slipping and sliding around on the floor. All that oil and broken glass made it hard for him to get up.

I jumped over him. As I was running out the back door, I had this weird feeling I was going to get in trouble for breaking the lamp. It was probably an antique. It might even have been van Wart's favorite for all I knew. Funny the stuff that goes through your head when someone's trying to kill you.

I ran out into the barnyard. I didn't know what to do next. Should I go to the log building? Untie Ms. Creaser and the bus driver? Let everyone out?

I could already hear the guy banging through the kitchen. There was no way I could get to them before he got to me. I had no time and no choices. I couldn't outrun him. He was a big guy. I jumped into the bus.

I was going to go for it. Get help. It was all I could do.

I'd never driven a bus before—I'd never driven anything before—but I couldn't let that stop me. I'd ridden *on* a bus every school day for the last ten years. I'd seen what the driver did. I could figure it out. I had to.

I slammed the door behind me. I jumped into the driver's seat. I stretched as far as I could to reach the pedals. The guy was right in front of the bus now. He was just standing there looking at me—laughing at me!

All of a sudden, I wasn't scared.

No, who am I kidding? I was still scared. But now I was mad too. I couldn't take one more person laughing at me. I was going to ram the guy down! He deserved it. I just had to start up the bus, and he'd be done for.

I leaned down to turn the key. It wasn't there.

I suddenly knew why the guy was laughing. He held up his hand and jangled the key chain at me.

The guy was really strong. I didn't have a chance. He dragged me over to the log house like I was a bag of garbage on my way to the curb. He tied me up beside Ms. Creaser. The rope cut into my wrists. He made sure of that.

"You okay?" Ms. Creaser said in this little voice.

I shook my head.

"Me neither," she said.

"That makes three of us," the bus driver croaked out.

Ms. Creaser and I both jumped.

"You're alive!" I said.

"Yeah—but not for long." It was the psycho guy who said that. He was smiling his face off, like he was so witty or something. Or maybe he was just smiling because he loved scaring people. He was certainly having a good time.

He slapped his hand against his face and made his eyes all big. They were really blue. It didn't help. He was still ugly.

"I forgot to tell you something, Teacher!" he said. He was pretending to be really sorry about it. "Part of your little tour includes a tragic accident. No extra charge, of course. In fact after the tragic accident, I'll even—you know—dispose of the bodies for free..."

Ms. Creaser sucked in her breath. She saw the kerosene. She saw the look on the guy's face. She put two and two together. She was terrified. You could tell.

Me? I was terrified too. But another part of me was so sick of the guy saying "tragic accident," I wanted to kill him. It was like he'd just learned what "tragic" meant and he had to show off by saying it over and over again. I felt like saying, "We get it, okay? We get it."

The guy picked up the can of kerosene.

He put on this really sucky voice and said, "Say your prayers!"

I said, "Accident victims don't usually die with their arms tied behind their backs."

It's always dangerous when I do that—you know, act like I have a brain. But what choice did I have?

I thought the guy was going to be mad—but he wasn't. He just shrugged. He was too stupid to be mad. He didn't understand what I was talking about.

"So what?" he said. "You're special!" He pinched my cheek—hard. "We're going to do it different for you." He smiled at his little joke and put the spout in the can.

"What I mean," I said, "is that nobody is going to believe it's an accident if we're all tied up."

Now the guy got it. Now he looked like he was going to hit me.

"Or if we're covered in bruises," I said. He held back. I don't know why. What was one more bruise now?

"They'll know it's murder," I said, "and they'll come looking for you. Your fingerprints must be everywhere. You can't burn the whole place down."

To tell the truth, I wasn't really sure about that last part. I mean, why *couldn't* he burn the whole place down? He had the matches.

The guy was twitching again. He reached into his pocket. I thought he was going for his cell phone, but he surprised me. He pulled out a gun.

He called me a name, then he dragged me up onto my feet. He untied my arms with his left hand. He stood back. He kept the gun aimed right at me. I was going to say that a bullet in the head wouldn't look like an accident either—but that might have bugged him so much he would have shot me anyway. I decided just to keep my mouth shut and do what he said. For a while, at least.

"Untie the others," he said.

The bus driver's knot came undone pretty easy, but I couldn't get Ms. Creaser untied. My hands were really shaking. I could tell the guy was getting mad that I was taking so long. That only made them shake worse. I finally pulled at the knot with my teeth. It worked, but I felt bad about leaving drool all over Ms. Creaser's wrist. I said sorry. She just shrugged like it was no big deal.

"Help them up," the guy said. He unlocked the door.

"Get in," he said. "*Now* say your prayers." He was smiling again.

"You better say yours too," I said. I was really asking for it now but, hey, it was a chance I had to take.

His eyes squinted up like he couldn't stand the sight of me. He twitched a bit, but he didn't shoot.

"If you light that match," I said, "you'll be the first to go up in flames. You're covered in kerosene from that lamp that I—you know—*accidentally* hit you with..."

The guy totally lost it. He lunged at us like some kind of crazed animal. He screamed, "GET IN! GET IN!" and shoved us through the door.

We fell in. There was a crunch when we hit the ground. That was the bus driver landing on top of me and Ms. Creaser. He weighed a ton.

The other kids all ran forward to help. The guy fired a shot in the air. The kids screamed. They left us where we were.

The guy slammed the door. We heard the lock clang shut.

chapter thirteen

Nothing happened for a couple of seconds. I guess people were waiting to make sure the guy was gone. Then everyone ran over to help. Or, more like it, to *be* helped.

Kids were crying and going, "What are we going to do, Ms. Creaser? What are we going to do?"

She tried to say something. Her voice was all groggy and messed up. She'd whacked her head on the ground again when she got pushed through the door. Some kids helped her sit up against the wall.

Nobody helped me. I don't think they even noticed I'd been gone. I got myself up.

It was dark inside the building. There were just a few streams of light coming in through little gaps in the roof. The place stunk of hay and manure and scared people.

It didn't take me long to realize that the grown-ups wouldn't be able to do much for us. Ms. Creaser was a mess. The bus driver's heart was acting up from all the stress. And Mr. van Wart—the real Mr. van Wart—had a broken arm. His wrist was bent into an *L*. My stomach flipped just looking at it.

I wasn't sure the kids would be able to help either. Most of them were huddled together in little groups, crying. Shane was just sitting in the corner by himself, like someone had given him a time-out. He didn't look very scary anymore. Sam DeMont—Mr. Popular—was on a rant about how it was the school's fault we were in this position. If the principal hadn't banned cell phones, none of this would ever have happened. We could have just called for help, he said. We'd be home now!

But we weren't home, and we didn't have cell phones. We were here in a dark, locked building waiting for a maniac to come back with a match.

I figured the guy was in the house, washing the kerosene off himself. I wondered how long that would take. Good thing van Wart didn't have running water. The guy would have to go out and pump some himself. I thought that should buy us a few extra minutes.

I wished people would stop weeping and wailing so I could think better—but that was one of the things I wasn't going to be able to change either. Sam was bugging me most of all. He kept going on and on about how it wasn't fair. How come the teachers got to have cell phones and we don't?

I felt like saying, "Who cares if the teachers have cell phones!" but I didn't. I thought about it for a second, and I said, "Hey..."

I ran over to Ms. Creaser. I shook her awake. I tried not to hurt her.

"Do you have a cell phone?" I said.

She nodded. My heart jumped. Maybe if I called 9-1-1, the cops would get here before the guy did. "It's on the bus," she said.

My heart jumped again, but this time it was in a bad way. I kind of wished the guy had just killed us and gotten it over with.

I couldn't stand there waiting for that to happen. I had to do something. I tried to be logical. What were our chances of getting out of here alive? I looked around. The door was locked. I knew that. I fumbled over and tried one of the windows. They were all boarded up tight.

"You won't be able to open them," someone said. "We tried that already."

I knew that voice. I heard it every night in my head when I tried to go to sleep. It was Shane. He sounded different now, though. This time, he didn't say, "You idiot" or "Pigboy" or anything. He was just telling me the facts—like we were two normal people having a conversation. It was weird.

I said, "Yeah, okay." I hated him less when he was scared.

I went over to van Wart. He was either in shock or being really brave. He was just sitting there, holding his bent-up arm. He wasn't moaning or crying like I'd be if my arm looked like that.

"Is there any other way out of here?" I said. "Like a trap door or something?"

He shook his head. What was I thinking? As if van Wart wouldn't have mentioned by now that there was a trap door!

"What about a place we could break through?" I said. "Like a weak spot somewhere?"

"No," he said. "I built this strong. I need it to be safe. I store my seeds here.

It's my warehouse." He actually said "varehouse" with a *v*. He really was Dutch after all.

He gave me this sad look. "I'm sorry," he said. I didn't know if he meant that he was sorry he'd done such a good job building it—or if he was sorry he'd invited us on this stupid field trip.

"You couldn't have known," I said. That worked whatever he meant.

I left him. I kicked some straw around. I tried to think of something on my own. There *had* to be a way out—other than the way the guy was planning for us, I mean.

I looked around where the little streams of light were shining on the ground. I only looked there because it was too dark to see much anywhere else.

I was, like, studying the floor when something just clicked in my brain. I knew what I was doing wrong.

I thought, "Idiot! Don't look down. Look up!"

The light was streaming in through

holes in the roof. Little holes. In other words, little openings to the outside. If I could get up to the roof, couldn't I just make them bigger holes? Holes that were big enough to climb through?

I ran back to Ms. Creaser.

"Your cell phone's where? Where in the bus?" I said.

I'm sure if her head hadn't hurt so much she would have asked what I was up to. Instead she just said, "In my purse."

"What does your purse look like?" I said.

It was hard for her to speak. I could tell. "Dark green," she said. "The phone... is in...the outside pocket...or...it's in the side pocket...the little one...next to...my make-up bag...or it's..." She went on and on. What is it with ladies and their purses? Do they really need all that stuff? I felt bad for her, but I finally just said, "Yeah, yeah. Don't worry. I'll find it."

I dragged a bunch of seed bags over to where the biggest stream of light was shining in. Nobody even bothered asking what I was doing. I climbed on top. My plan was to grab the rafters and swing myself up.

It didn't take me long to realize it wasn't a good plan. There was no way I was strong enough to swing my puny body anywhere.

The guy was going to be back any minute. I knew that. I had to move fast. I had to swallow my pride.

"Shane," I said. "Can you help me?"

chapter fourteen

I hated to ask, but Shane's the biggest kid in our class. I knew it wouldn't be any trouble for him to pick me up. I'd imagined it many times—Shane hurling me off cliffs, into ditches, over walls, you name it.

He said, "Sure. What do you want me to help you with?" He sounded like a regular Boy Scout.

"Lift me up onto the rafters," I said. He climbed onto the seed bags and hoisted me up over his head like I was crowd-surfing at a rave. He said, "Geez, you're some skinny," but that's all. It wasn't so bad.

I got my feet on his shoulders for balance and pulled myself flat onto the rafter. I slid on my belly to the hole in the roof. I was glad it was so dark. I didn't have to worry about looking down and getting scared. I wouldn't have seen much, anyway.

I started yanking at the roof shingles with my hands. I was pulling off pieces about the size of tortilla chips. It would be ages before even a runt like me could get through the hole.

I felt a tap on my shoulder. It was the handle of a shovel. "Try this," Shane said.

I stuck the end of the shovel through the hole. I leaned the pole against the rafter and pushed down. It worked like a little lever. A big piece of roof cracked off. I almost fell over when it gave way. I got my balance and tried again. A bit more came off. Most of it hit me right in the face. I spit out the shingles and gave the roof one more good crack. The opening was about the size of a toilet seat hole now.

The sun shone in and made a spotlight on the floor. Kids weren't crying anymore—at least not much. They were all trying to see what I was doing.

"I'm going out," I said.

I loved the way that sounded. It was just like what the heroes say in war movies right before they hurl themselves out of the plane. I felt like I should wink and say something like, "See you around, guys" and be really cool about it—but who was I kidding? I wasn't cool. I'd just sound like an idiot.

Instead I said, "I'll try to do something. Like stop him or something. If you keep working at the hole, maybe you guys can get out too."

Shane said, "Yeah. Thanks. We'll try." He didn't look too confident. He must have known it would take at least an hour to make a hole big enough for him to get through.

I pushed out through the roof. It was a tight squeeze even for me—and I was the scrawniest kid in my class, by a mile. I got my head and shoulders out, but the rough edges of the hole scraped my belly and got caught on my pants. I pulled and squirmed, but it didn't do any good. I was stuck. Time was ticking away. I did what I had to do.

I used my feet to rub my shoes off. I unzipped my pants.

Of course this was not the day that I chose to wear the boxers that my half-sister gave me for Christmas. Like I said, I'm not a lucky person. This was the day I was wearing the tighty-whities that my mother always gets me. The pair I had on was about five years old and practically see-through.

I didn't really care. I just whipped off my jeans and pushed myself through the hole. I can just imagine what Shane thought when they landed on the floor.

Pigboy

I was already falling from the roof before it dawned on me that it was a long way to the ground.

chapter fifteen

There was a cart full of hay right below me. (My mother would say, "See! You are a lucky person." She'd totally ignore the fact that a crazy guy was trying to kill me.) I clipped my head on the rails when I landed, but I was okay. I found my glasses and scrambled to my feet. I was a little cold in just my underpants, but I didn't have to worry. I heated up pretty fast.

My plan was to get the cell phone, call

9-1-1 again, then somehow stop the guy before he set fire to the building.

How?

I hadn't worked that out yet.

I landed at the back of the building. I sneaked around to the front. I checked to make sure the coast was clear, then I ran to the bus. I yanked open the door. Stuff was all over the place. How was I ever going to find Ms. Creaser's purse?

I kicked things out of my way. A blue purse. A brown one. A green one! There it is.

I started rooting around through the front pocket like she said. No cell phone. I dumped some junk out. Which side pocket did she mean? The purse was covered in them. I was scared and I was mad again. I didn't need another problem right now.

The kitchen door slammed. The guy came out. He was clean and dressed in new clothes. He barely looked psycho. He looked like a farmer going on a date.

He must have managed to get the

kerosene off. There was nothing to stop him now. I didn't have time to find the cell phone! I was just going to have to go. I grabbed the purse and threw the strap over my shoulder. I'd look for the cell phone later. Right now, I needed a weapon. I did a fast scan of the bus.

Was I crazy? There wouldn't be any weapons here! Like a teacher was going to let us bring weapons on a field trip? No way. I'd have to find something in the barnyard.

No. I wouldn't have time for that either. The guy was almost at the log house. I had to stop him. I had to stop him any way I could.

I ran out of the bus.

"Yoo-hoo!" I said. "Yoo-hoo! Over here!"

He turned around and saw me.

"You!" he screamed.

Boy, if looks could kill.

The guy clearly wasn't thinking straight. He's got twenty-nine kids locked up in a building. He's standing right beside it with the kerosene and a box of matches.

You'd think he'd just light the place on fire while he could.

No.

Instead he drops the matches and takes off after the one kid who's not locked up. Me.

I was really bugging him now. I could tell. He was wild. It wasn't just that I'd managed to get out. It was something more than that. He was running with his shoulders hunched up and his bottom lip pushed out and this look of pure hate on his face.

He started screaming at me. At first I couldn't understand him. I was halfway round the side of the barn before I realized what he was saying.

He kept going, "Where are your pants?" It was like that was all he could think about.

If I hadn't been running so hard—if I hadn't been so totally scared out of my mind—I probably would have laughed. He was mad at me for being outside in my underwear! Who knows what he thought about the purse? It's like I'd insulted him or something. Like I was making fun of him.

I think that's what really got him. Here he was trying to be serious—I mean, what's more serious than setting a house full of kids on fire?—and I was goofing around in my underwear! He was going to kill me when he got his hands on me. I barely even felt the rocks jamming into my sock feet. I was just flying. I skidded around the corner of the barn. I had this idea I could hide there and ambush him. Hit him over the head with a shovel or something when he came around the corner.

It wasn't going to happen. There wasn't going to be any ambush here. I couldn't see a shovel anywhere. The pigs were squealing so loud I couldn't think straight. I had to do something. The guy was going to be there any second.

With his gun.

I'd forgotten he had a gun. Suddenly this whole stopping him thing seemed like a dumb idea. Why didn't I just stay in the bus while I had a chance? I had to do something fast.

I opened the pigpen and jumped in. Mud and manure and whatever else it was splashed up to my neck and splattered over my glasses. I dove to the back. I lay down flat. The pigs all crowded around me, sniffing and snorting. They were fascinated. I hoped they'd stay fascinated until he was gone.

The guy came tearing around the corner. He stopped. He looked around. "I know you're here somewhere," he said. He had that jokey tone in his voice again. He started creeping toward the pigpen. I grabbed the only weapon I had.

Manure.

I jumped up from behind this big porker and winged a handful right at him. It was gross. I got him right in the face. It must have come as a shock. He dropped his gun.

I couldn't let him find it. I just kept chucking stuff at him. He was cursing and swearing. He put his arms up trying to cover his face. I was creaming him. Terror really gives you a lot of energy.

It also apparently gets pigs all wound up. They were squealing and shrieking and crawling all over each other like they were at a rock concert.

I was screaming too. I hope I was screaming like a warrior charging into battle—but I know I wasn't. I was just screaming like a terrified kid. I was screeching and throwing as fast and hard as I could. I must have looked nuts.

I don't really know what happened next. I guess the guy just couldn't stand it anymore. He suddenly, like, growled and then just lunged at me.

There was one thing he hadn't counted on. To tell you the truth, I hadn't counted on it either. I don't know if it was because they liked me. Or if they were afraid of him. Or if they just noticed that the gate was open and decided to get out while the going was good.

Who knows?

But when the guy lunged at me—the hogs lunged right back at him. There was this giant squeal and they charged. One little piglet got him just below the knees. The guy's feet went flying out from under him. He went, "AAAAAAAA!" His head hit the ground. There was this big splat of manure. And then nothing else.

The guy was out cold.

chapter sixteen

I grabbed the gun. I put it in Ms. Creaser's purse. I left this big porker practically sitting on the guy. I ran over to the log house. I banged on the door. I screamed, "Don't worry. It's okay. I'll be back." I took the rope the guy used to tie me up.

I ran back to the pigpen. I rolled the guy over and tied his hands behind his back. I sat him up and tied him to the fence. I used about thirty knots. He wasn't going anywhere. He moaned and opened his eyes. He started swearing at me like you wouldn't believe.

I ran. I was still scared of him, even tied up. I couldn't handle him screaming like that. I really didn't want to hear what he was going to do with me as soon as he got free. I went to the bus. I got my duct tape. I went back and taped the guy's mouth shut. After that, he didn't freak me out so much. I knew that duct tape would come in handy, sooner or later.

I was in front of the barn, rooting around through Ms. Creaser's purse looking for her cell phone when I heard this loud noise.

Sirens. Lots of sirens. The police were here.

I told them what had happened. They got the kids out. They arrested the guy.

We were halfway home before I realized I should probably put some pants on.

chapter seventeen

That 9-1-1 operator had figured everything out. She heard me say "van Wart," found the address and sent the cops. There'd been a prison break that afternoon. The police were already looking for the guy.

Or should I say they were already looking for Archibald James Dobbin—armed robber, car thief and general all-round psycho. He's also—thanks to our little field trip—a lifer. He's never getting out of prison again.

His friend—Kyle Jason Fiske—is in trouble too. He was the guy who hid the gun and the cell phone on the farm. He got six years for "aiding and abetting" a criminal. The judge also gave him a few extra years for coming up with the whole "tragic accident" idea.

I managed to get my picture in the paper. The good part is that they made it sound like I was some big hero. The bad part is that they used this stupid headline— "Boy goes Hogg-wild!" They also had to mention, of course, that I was wearing underpants and a lady's purse. I found it really embarrassing, but my mother loved it. She said I did the Hoggs proud.

She bought me new glasses and a week's worth of boxer shorts. She threw my old briefs in the rag bag.

Mr. van Wart had to have his arm operated on, but it looks like it's going to work okay. He was really thankful for what I did. He gave my mother a whole bunch of pork sausages. They came from one of the pigs that lunged at the guy. That didn't seem fair to me, but they tasted okay.

Mr. Benvie goes out on the weekends with a bunch of volunteers and helps keep the farm going. He's trying to arrange another field trip there for the spring. He thinks it would be good for us. Help give us "closure." I told him I'm allergic to hay.

The bus driver retired. He and his wife moved to Florida.

Ms. Creaser had a concussion. She had to stay in hospital for a couple of days. We all went in to see her. She said she was going to quit teaching and go into something less dangerous—"like working for the bomb squad, for instance." We all laughed.

Shane doesn't bug me anymore. In fact he even thanked me for what I did. He usually calls me Dan now. He sometimes forgets and calls me Pigboy, but he says it in a nice way.

None of that means we're friends of course.

Why would we be? We don't have anything to build a friendship on. We lost the one and only thing we had in common.

Ever since that stupid field trip, neither of us hates Dan Hogg.

Vicki Grant is the popular author of many books for young people, including *Dead End Job*, *The Puppet Wrangler*, and *Quid Pro Quo*, winner of the 2006 Arthur Ellis award for best juvenile novel from Crime Writers of Canada, an Edgar Allen Poe Award nominee and New York Public Library Books for Teen Age list selection. Vicki lives in Halifax, Nova Scotia.

Other titles in the Orca Currents series

Visit www.orcabook.com for more information.

Other Orca Currents Novels

Laggan Lard Butts by Eric Walters

"That was the bravest thing I ever saw in my whole life," Tanner said.

"Not that brave."

"You're like my hero," Taylor agreed.

"Big deal. It doesn't mean anything. Now we just get to spend more time trying to get people to vote for something that has no chance of winning."

"No chance?" Tanner demanded.

"Yes, no chance."

"I don't believe my ears," Taylor said. "Didn't you listen to the announcements today? A quitter never wins and a Lard Butt never quits. Go, Lard Butts!"

Other Orca Currents Novels

Dog Walker by Karen Spafford-Fitz

"Just one question, Turk," Mom says. "Why didn't you tell us sooner?"

Mom must have read another parenting article. I can almost see the headline: Getting Your Teen to Open Up to You.

"Well, er...I wanted to get my business running before I said anything. And," I put on my most innocent face, "I had this crazy idea you might think my business was something shady, stupid, or immoral."

I can't tell for sure, but I think Mom and Dad almost look ashamed.

Yes!